MY GRANDPA IS A DINOSAUR

RICHARD FAIRGRAY TERRY JONES

Coloring by Tara Black

Sky Pony Press
New York

For Paul Eiding, a grandpa who will one day be a dinosaur.

Sky Pony Press books may be purchased in bulk at special discounts for sales promotion, corporate gifts, fund-raising, or educational purposes. Special editions can also be created to specifications. For details, contact the Special Sales Department, Sky Pony Press, 307 West 36th Street, 11th Floor, New York, NY 10018 or info@skyhorsepublishing.com.

Sky Pony® is a registered trademark of Skyhorse Publishing, Inc.®, a Delaware corporation.

Visit our website at www.skyponypress.com.

10 9 8 7 6 5 4 3 2 1

Manufactured in China, January 2016
This product conforms to CPSIA 2008

Library of Congress Cataloging-in-Publication Data is available on file.

Cover design and illustration by Richard Fairgray

Print ISBN: 978-1-63450-632-8
Ebook ISBN: 978-1-63450-633-5

Wanda knew there was something odd about her family,
and it wasn't her older sister.

It wasn't her bratty brother.

It wasn't even her mom or dad.

The thing that was so odd about Wanda's family . . .

was that her grandpa was a dinosaur.

All his pants had to have tail holes.

At the Grandparents' Day picnic he was the only one who ate an entire tree.

And paleontologists were always following his footprints.

Wanda's parents even had to put in a special car seat for him.

And when he jumped in the pool he splashed out all the water.

Not to mention that on every Hallowe'en he dressed as the ghost of a dinosaur.

But the oddest part of all was that no one would believe Wanda when she told them about her grandpa.

Wanda tried to tell her sister.

But her sister didn't believe her.

Wanda tried to tell her friend.

But her friend didn't believe her, either.

But even her mom didn't believe her.

So Wanda decided to ask him herself.

For the rest of the day Wanda and her grandpa had more fun together than they had ever had.

And that afternoon, when her grandpa took her back to his retirement home, Wanda realized . . .

that her grandpa wasn't the only dinosaur around.

Not even close.